FU-DOG

RUMER GODDEN

FU-DOG

PICTURES BY VALERIE LITTLEWOOD

VIKING

VIKING
Published by the Penguin Group
Viking Penguin, a division of Penguin Books USA Inc.,
40 West 23rd Street, New York, New York 10010, U.S.A.
Penguin Books Ltd, 27 Wrights Lane, London W8 5TZ, England
Penguin Books Australia Ltd, Ringwood, Victoria, Australia
Penguin Books Canada Ltd, 2801 John Street, Markham, Ontario, Canada L3R 1B4
Penguin Books (N.Z.) Ltd, 182–190 Wairau Road, Auckland 10, New Zealand

Penguin Books Ltd, Registered Offices: Harmondsworth, Middlesex, England

First published in Great Britain by Julia MacRae Books, a division of Walker Books Ltd, 1989

First American edition published in 1990
1 3 5 7 9 10 8 6 4 2

Library of Congress Catalog Card Number: 89-50858
ISBN: 0-670-82300-7

Printed in Hong Kong
Set in Goudy Old Style

For Charles

R.G.

For Jessie and Charlie

V.L.

I

"He's hideous," said Malcolm.

"He's beautiful," said Li-la, "but what is he?"

He had come to Li-la in a parcel wrapped in fine red tissue paper that smelled "of spices," said Mum sniffing it. He was perhaps four inches long, made of green satin with golden flowers on it, a gold line showing where his backbone was. His eyes were pearls with a black middle; they stuck out as if they were on stalks. He had a wide scarlet mouth with white teeth, two large ones like fangs at the side and a row between, but he seemed to be smiling. His nose was painted dark red. He had three horns on his head in black and gold; his ears either side had white fur edges and he had a white fur ruff, with more white fur round his tail. One dark green paw was on a ball made of satin in bright colours. No wonder the children had never seen anything like him.

"What is he?"

"He's a Fu-dog," said Mum. "Long long ago in China,

Fu-dogs used to guard the temples and palaces, that's why he looks a little like a dragon."

"Will he guard us?" asked Li-la.

"I'm sure he will," said Mum.

"Stuff! He's only four inches long," said Malcolm.

"He isn't only four inches long." Li-la did not know then why she said that. All the same, she wished Fu-dog was real.

Great Uncle had sent Fu-dog. In the children's house Great Uncle was always spoken of with respect because their family was not quite the same as the families of other children in St. Mary's Green, the quiet little village in Devon where they lived.

Great Uncle was Chinese. His sister, who had been Mum's mother, was Chinese too, but she had married an Englishman so that Mum, Mrs. Smith, was half-Chinese; she had married Dad, Mr. Smith, another Englishman, so that Malcolm and Li-la were a quarter-Chinese.

It was Great Uncle who had given Li-la her Chinese name – Dad had wanted to call her Mary after Mum. Li-la suited her much better. Dad was fair, big and tall; Mum looked like any English mum, and Malcolm had fair hair like Dad's though his eyes were darker than most English boys'. But Li-la's hair was black, cut short in a fringe, her black eyes were slant and her skin was like a white-heart cherry that has a tinge of yellow in its pink.

"I like my funny eyes," said Li-la. "I think I've got a dear little face."

Most people thought so too but Dad sighed. He did not like Mum's family. "Too pernickity for me," said Dad.

"They're not pernickity." Though Li-la did not know what pernickity meant, she did not like Mum to be sad.

"I'm afraid Dad's too rough and ready for them," Mum sighed too.

"He isn't rough and ready," said Malcolm at once.

"I should so much like to see Great Uncle and Big Brother," said Mum.

Mum had not seen her brother since her wedding. "Not for eleven years," more years than even Li-la could imagine; nor could she imagine what it would be like not to see Malcolm every day.

Great Uncle had come once for the christening.

"Was that when Dad was rough and ready?" Li-la asked.

"I'm afraid so," said Mum.

"Why didn't Great Uncle come to *my* christening?" asked Malcolm. "I'm the eldest."

"Well, in China boys are important," said Mum who always tried to keep things even, "so important that they don't need extra attention."

"Do I get extra attention?" asked Li-la.

"You know you do," said Mum. "Look at all the presents Great Uncle has sent you."

Great Uncle had never come again but every year, on Li-la's birthday, he had sent a present. Now there was a whole shelf of them and all of them were Chinese.

There was a model of a Chinese town in pink and white and green plaster, houses with tip-tilted roofs that curled up at the edges, pagodas that were like graceful little towers and were hung with tiny bells; a little curved bridge had a fishing boat below it that looked like the boat on a willow-pattern plate; a little man fished from it with a tiny fishing-rod and line that had, on the end of it, a still tinier silver fish. One

birthday there was a tree, twelve inches high, its stem and branches of gold wire with flowers of white mother-of-pearl and red coral. "'It must be very precious," said Mum; Li-la hardly dared to touch it. There was a figure in ivory of an old Chinese man sitting on a little carved wood throne; he wore a blue robe — it looked like a long tunic; his hair was ivory white and he had a delicately carved pointed beard. "He's a mandarin," said Mum and before Li-la could ask, "a Chinese nobleman," explained Mum.

"Is Great Uncle a mandarin?" asked Li-la.

"Don't be silly. He keeps a restaurant," said Malcolm.

"Well, does he wear a blue robe?"

"Don't be silly. He's a business man so he must wear business men's clothes," but Li-la liked to think of Great Uncle in a blue robe and as a mandarin. This year the best present of all had come, Fu-dog. "But I wish you were real," Li-la told him.

"I am real," said Fu-dog. She heard him clearly though no-one else did, not even Malcolm, especially not Malcolm. "I am real," said Fu-dog. "I have been real for more than two thousand years."

"Crikey!" said Li-la, "I've only been real for seven!"

Dad worked as foreman in a big factory that made Devonshire jams and jellies. "It's I who keeps the jam bubbling," he said. Li-la imagined the factory full of great vats of red, green and purple berry jam — apricot was her favourite — all hissing and bubbling under Dad's care, with orange vats of marmalade and ruby redcurrant jelly but then, "Li-la can imagine anything," said Malcolm.

"Fu-dog likes being here," she told Malcolm. "He's wagging." Malcolm did not like Fu-dog being here; it was as if he had come between him, Malcolm, and Li-la, the little sister who had always done exactly what her brother told her. Now, "Don't take Fu-dog to school. They'll laugh at him," Malcolm told her but Li-la took him to school next day and, "Nobody laughed," said Li-la. The children had taken it in turns to hold him and the teacher had stood him on her desk.

"Fu-dog should be kept on the shelf with the other Chinese things," said Malcolm but Li-la made him not a kennel but a temple out of their cardboard toy theatre – Fu-dog was too big for the model Chinatown; his eating bowl was the gold top from a milk bottle and his drinking bowl Mum's silver thimble which she never used. When Mum was baking, Li-la begged a little piece of dough and used the thimble to make tiny rounds for dog biscuits.

"What do Chinese people like to eat?" she asked Mum.

"Noodles," said Mum, "and rice, especially fried rice. Crispy fried seaweed…"

"Seaweed?"

"Yes. It tastes lovely. Prawns and duck with bamboo shoots. Egg Fuey. Pork with sweet-and-sour sauce and black bean sauce – but Dad doesn't like Chinese food," said Mum wistfully.

"Nor do I," said Malcolm who had never tasted it; none of these wonderful sounding things were in Mum's kitchen.

"They're very fond of pork," said Mum, "pork with dumplings," and Li-la rolled bread into balls the size of peas for dumplings and cut up snippets of meat, hoping Fu-dog

would think they were dumplings and pork.

"Look. He's wagging," she told Malcolm.

"Wagging his head, instead of his tail!" said Malcolm in scorn. "I told you, the Chinese are topsy-turvy, upside down, back to front."

It is true that Chinese people read from right to left, not left to right; their books start at the back and read through to the front. To the Chinese, Malcolm's name should not have been Malcolm Smith, but Smith Malcolm and, "I should have been Dog-fu instead of Fu-dog but if Fu – me – comes first it is so much nicer," said Fu-dog.

Li-la thought so too; she liked Fu-dog wagging his head instead of his tail and she said, "Perhaps Chinese people think it's we who are topsy-turvy, upside down, back to front."

"Stuff!" said Malcolm.

2

Every day Li-la grew more and more curious about Great Uncle. She asked questions. "No-one has ever asked as many questions as Li-la!" said Malcolm.

"Does Great Uncle live in China?" she asked Mum.

"Well, he lives in Chinatown."

"Where's Chinatown?"

"Every big city has its Chinatown," said Mum. "Great Uncle's is in London."

Li-la tried to imagine it but all she could imagine was her model town grown big, real houses with tip-tilted curled up roofs, tall pagodas, golden-stemmed trees with white and red flowers lining the streets; a bridge. "Is there a lake in London?" she asked Mum. "Lots of lakes," so the little man in the fishing boat would be there; perhaps he caught silver fish for Great Uncle's restaurant, thought Li-la. She imagined a temple full size, with its courtyard and Fu-dog to guard it.

"But you wouldn't be big enough," she told him.

Fu-dog was offended. "I can be as big as the sky, which I can fill," he boasted.

"How?" asked Li-la.

"Hold me up to your eye and look," and it was true; when Li-la held him up to her eye, he was all she could see, not even a patch of sky.

"If I want to make myself small, I can go in your sleeve," said Fu-dog and Li-la found he could easily fit in her sleeve; soon she took him everywhere she went. *If only you were really real*, Li-la still could not help thinking.

Perhaps it was having Fu-dog that made her long so much for a real dog but not an ordinary dog, thought Li-la. Could there be a real dog like Fu-dog? she wondered. "Tell me," she asked Fu-dog, "what is a Chinese real dog like?"

"You should call them Peking dogs," said Fu-dog. "Peking is a royal city and they are royal dogs. They belonged to the Empress."

"You're making it up," said Malcolm when Li-la told him this.

"How could I make it up?" asked Li-la. "I didn't even know what an Empress was."

"What's an Empress?" she had asked Fu-dog.

"A Queen of Queens. No-one else was allowed to have Peking dogs!"

"But what were they like?"

Fu-dog began to chant as if he were speaking for the Empress:

"'Let the Peking dog be small,

"'Let it have a ruff around its neck' – like mine," said Fu-dog breaking off.

"'Let its coat be plentiful, its feet tufted. Let its tail fall like a chrysanthemum with full petals...

"'Let its nose be flat' – like mine," said Fu-dog.

"I hope it doesn't have his terrible teeth," said Malcolm.

"Malcolm can't talk," said Fu-dog, and it was true that Malcolm's teeth – his second ones had just come through – looked too big in his boy's face.

What Malcolm liked least of all was that he could not hear Fu-dog talk. Li-la had to tell him what he said. She faithfully told him everything but, "I'm the eldest, why can't *I* hear him?" said Malcolm.

"Perhaps you will one day but not yet," said Fu-dog and went on, chanting:

"'Let the Peking dog's eyes be dark, large and shining.

"'Let it be lively and gambol.

"'Let it be friendly...'"

"Oh, I do so want one!" said Li-la.

"'Let its colour be red, apricot, black, white or gold.'"

"I like gold best," said Li-la.

"They can be called, 'golden-coated nimble dogs'," said Fu-dog.

"What's nimble?"

"Light and quick."

"Oh, I wish I had a golden-coated nimble dog," cried Li-la.

"When the Empress had them," said Fu-dog, "she wrote all their names on a scroll."

"What's a scroll?"

"A long, long piece of writing."

"Back to front," jeered Malcolm when Li-la told him.

"Back to front with paintings," Fu-dog said with dignity.

"It had to be long; it is called the Scroll of a Hundred Pekingese."

"A *hundred*!"

"The Empress had a hundred Peking dogs."

"Couldn't she spare just one?" asked Li-la.

"Great Uncle must be very rich," said Malcolm, "to send Li-la all these things."

"Well," said Mum, "they say everything Great Uncle touches turns to gold."

"*Really?*" asked Li-la. It seemed Great Uncle could do anything and a new thought came to Li-la, an exciting thought: if Great Uncle touched Fu-dog, would Fu-dog turn into a golden-coated nimble dog?

"Fu-dog," she said, "we must go and see Great Uncle at once."

From the house the children could see trains coming and going in the valley below. Fu-dog had seen them when Li-la put him on the window sill.

"Where are they going to?" Li-la would ask and Malcolm always answered, "To London."

London's Chinatown, thought Li-la.

"I haven't been in a train," said Fu-dog, "except in a parcel." Li-la could tell he was pleased because he wagged his head. "Wrong end," Malcolm would have said.

"Mum, can we go in a train to see Great Uncle?" but Mum only said, "One day," and Li-la did not like 'one day'; she wanted it to be today.

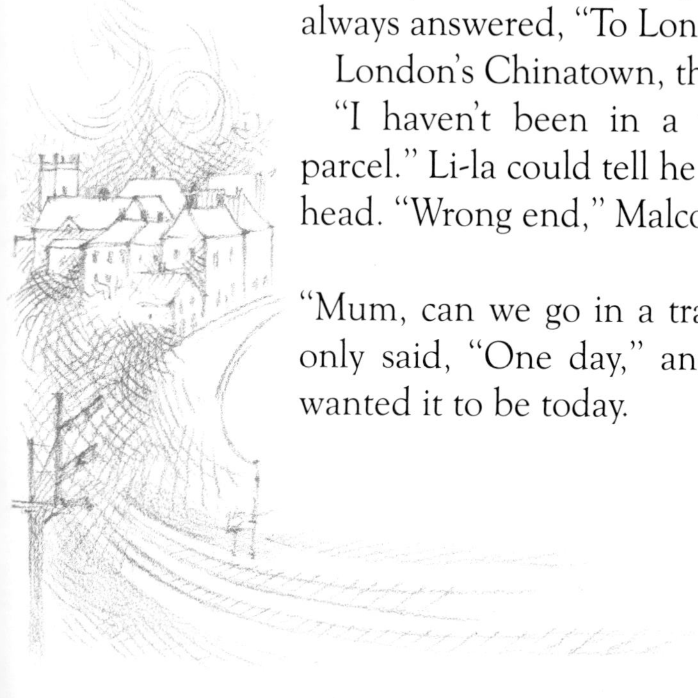

"I will take you," said Fu-dog. "Why not? The ball under my paw is supposed to be the world so I can take you all over the world."

"I don't want to go all over the world," said Li-la, "I want to go to London Chinatown." She still seemed to see the pink tip-tilted roofs of its houses, the pagodas, the pool and the streets of flowering trees. "London Chinatown," said Li-la.

"I'll take you," said Fu-dog again, "you can ride on my back." Li-la did not like to remind him he was no more than four inches long — she knew Fu-dog often thought he was bigger than he was — and perhaps he is, thought Li-la. "I'll take you," said Fu-dog and Li-la only said, "I think we'd better take Malcolm."

She did not say, "Malcolm will take us," but, "*We'll* take Malcolm."

"I don't want to go to Chinatown," said Malcolm. Then he thought again, "I wouldn't mind going to London." All at once the full meaning of Li-la's idea came to him. "Go without *telling*?" he asked. "Without Mum! Without even Mum?"

"Yes, but...how could we?" asked Li-la.

"Easily." Once he understood, Malcolm was fired and, "Easily," he said. Like the other boys in St. Mary's Green, Malcolm often went down to the railway station with a notebook and pencil train-spotting and he knew all about trains. "It's only four hours to London," he said. "We could be there before we were missed. But," and his face clouded. "what about Dad?"

They were both silent — Dad would not be pleased — then,

"I know," said Li-la, "I'll ask Fu-dog."

What Fu-dog said was so unexpected she hardly dared tell Malcolm. "Dad will be glad," said Fu-dog.

Malcolm, strangely, did not say 'Stuff', and Li-la guessed that now he wanted so much to go to London he had decided it was better not to think about Dad. "We'll have to buy tickets," he said instead.

"I've got a pound," said Li-la, "and four pence."

"That's not enough."

"There's lots of money in your pig."

Malcolm's pig was a china pig money-box. "That's for my bicycle." Malcolm's bicycle was the pivot of his dreams. A red bicycle with white tyres and three speeds.

"Great Uncle will buy you a bicycle." Malcolm did not believe it but he opened his money-pig.

"We'll have to wait for the right day."

"In China we always wait for the right day," said Fu-dog.

The very next morning when Li-la woke up, Fu-dog, in his temple kennel, was wagging.

"Is this the day?" Li-la asked.

Fu-dog nodded. "The auspicious day."

"What's auspicious?"

"Very, very lucky," said Fu-dog, which was right. To begin with it was a school holiday and then at breakfast the telephone rang; when Mum came back, "That was Mrs. Thompson," she said and sounded disappointed. "She has tickets for a concert in town and wanted me to go with her, do a little shopping and have lunch first, but Dad's away all day and with you two..."

"We can go to Granny," Malcolm said quickly. That was quite usual. They often went to Granny – she was always there. "Our English grandmother," Li-la told Fu-dog, "Dad's mother."

"So you could," said Mum, relieved. "I'll ring Mrs. Thompson back but I'll have to hurry. She's catching the half-past nine bus."

"We'll wash up." Malcolm was unusually helpful.

"And tidy the house," Li-la joined in.

"Give Granny this note," said Mum when she was ready. "Tell her I'm sorry I didn't warn her. I've asked her to give you your lunch and tea. I'll be back to fetch you. Lock the door and put the key under the mat. Wrap up warm – goodbye."

"Goodbye."

Of course the children did not go to Granny but dressed themselves carefully, Malcolm in his best jersey and cords and his new anorak. As Li-la was going to see Great Uncle, she thought she should wear a dress — and chose one with daisies on it; she wore warm white tights, red shoes with silver buckles and a red bow on her hair. She could not tie it very well; Malcolm tried but it was still askew. Her new anorak had bright colours, but Malcolm would not have anything but brown; they both had hoods with fur edgings — "like Fu-dog's ruff," said Li-la. When they were ready they went straight to the station.

"Two half fares to London." Malcolm said at the ticket office.

"And a dog ticket," whispered Li-la.

"Don't be silly," hissed Malcolm and Fu-dog stopped wagging.

"*Need* we take Malcolm?" he had asked Li-la.

"*Need* we take Fu-dog?" Malcolm had asked.

"Are you travelling alone?" the ticket man asked. It seemed he was going to be difficult. Oh these grown-ups! thought Malcolm. He did not know what to say until, at that moment, Li-la lifted her sleeve, Fu-dog looked out and, "We're travelling with Mr. Fu," said Malcolm. Li-la laughed with delight and, "Oh, well," said the ticket man. He let them through.

The train came in and it was not at all like a toy train; Li-la had not dreamed it could be so big, noisy and clanking, nor had Fu-dog; he nearly tumbled out of her sleeve in consternation. "It's a monster!" Then he thought again. "It's a dragon," and, like a true Fu-dog, remembered he was half-dragon himself and, "Cousin!" cried Fu-dog to the train though in a rather trembling voice. To Li-la, "The train is my cousin," he said.

"Only four hours to London," Malcolm had told them. At first they had been busy looking at the countryside that seemed to be flying past the window: fields and farms, cows, sheep, orchards, houses, villages, towns, roads with cars and people; even the clouds in the sky seemed to be flying. "Wah!" said Fu-dog – Li-la had put him by the window. They stopped at stations where Malcolm jumped down on the platform and took out his notebook with its worn-down pencil to spot other trains. "You'll be left behind," one old lady told him. Li-la thought so too and each time stood by the carriage door in terror.

Soon the time seemed to become very long, then felt longer and longer. "I'm hungry," said Li-la. "I'm thirsty."

There was a buffet car on the train; they went along the corridor to see. It had delicious things to eat: sausage rolls, sizzling toasted sandwiches, buttered rolls, chocolate bars, ice-cream, fizzy lemonade and orange squash, but Malcolm had only taken the ticket money out of his pig and used Li-la's pound as well so that they had nothing left but her four pennies and what could you buy at a buffet for four pence? "Nothing," said Li-la in disgust.

3

"This isn't London. It can't be!"

When they got out of the train, the station had seemed to the children like a horrible dark cavern full of noise and smells. "Trains and trains and trains," said Malcolm, for once too many for him. Even Fu-dog went back into Li-la's sleeve. There were hundreds of people, all carrying luggage, some pushing trolleys, so many people that the children were swept along, up a long ramp, across a wide space, full of more noise, people and luggage, down steps until they were out on a street of tall dark houses. There was only a glimpse of sky, snowflakes were beginning to come down. The pavements were thronged with people, most of them hurrying, while the road was packed with more cars than any of them, even Malcolm, had seen or imagined. Great red buses roared. "More dragons. Wah!" said Fu-dog who had come out of Li-la's sleeve. There was a stench of petrol and a cold wind blew litter round their ankles while, in the throb and roar of the traffic, they could hardly hear themselves speak.

"*This* isn't London." Li-la had not told Malcolm about her Chinatown London – it was her secret – but where was it? Where could it be in this noise and dirtiness? She was beginning to feel tears trickling down her cheek.

"We shouldn't have come," said Malcolm.

"We have come." It was Fu-dog's voice. His head was wagging. "What are those cars like black lacquer boxes" – lacquer is shiny – "on wheels, with a glow-worm on top?" asked Fu-dog.

"A *glow-worm*?" asked Li-la.

"Little insects, like a little beetle that can light up and shine. In China, boys and girls catch them and put them in cages made of grass stems, and carry them at night for insect lanterns. Look, there's one of them."

Li-la looked. Sure enough there were cars with lights on their roofs. As she looked, a gentleman stopped on the edge of the pavement, put up his hand, signalling, and one of these cars drew up, stopped beside him and he got in. "Catch a glow-worm car, Malcolm," cried Li-la, "ask him to take us to Great Uncle."

"Glow-worm car?" asked Malcolm. "You mean a taxi."

"Where to?" asked the taxi-driver, leaning round to open the door.

"Take us to the Chinese restaurant," said Malcolm. Li-la added, "Please."

The driver looked at them. "*The* Chinese restaurant, did you say?"

"Yes."

"Son," said the driver, "there are a hundred, maybe two

hundred, maybe a thousand Chinese restaurants in London."

Malcolm was a proud boy and his face turned red. How could he have known? St. Mary's Green had no restaurant at all, only a café. In the town where Mum had gone to meet Mrs. Thompson there was an Italian restaurant and an Indian curry one but only one of each; no Chinese restaurants at all.

"Which Chinese restaurant?" asked the driver.

"It belongs to our Chinese Great Uncle," said Li-la.

"And what's your Chinese Great Uncle's name?"

They could not answer because, now Malcolm and Li-la came to think of it, neither of them knew Great Uncle's name; they had not thought to ask Mum. "*I* couldn't be expected to know," said Fu-dog. To them Great Uncle was, simply, Great Uncle. "There are probably a thousand Chinese great uncles in London, if not five thousand," said the taxi-driver. "I think I had better take you to the police station."

"No! Oh, no!" and, "We'd better run," Malcolm was just going to say when, "Hold on!" said the taxi-driver.

He had caught sight of Fu-dog whom Li-la had taken out of her sleeve so that he could see the glow-worm car. "Would your Great Uncle's restaurant have two dragon sort of dogs outside it like that?" asked the driver.

"It could have," said Malcolm.

"Well, there's one near Piccadilly."

"Is that Chinatown?" asked Li-la.

"Could be," said the driver. "All right. We'll try there first. Hop in."

"He called me dragon dog," said Fu-dog. "He must be a well-informed driver," and he wagged hard.

Again it seemed a long way, through streets even more crowded, though here there were shops and bright lights, even more people. "Wah!" Fu-dog said again when Li-la held him up to see. There was no sign of a curly roof, a pagoda or flowering tree. Li-la did not feel at all like saying, "Wah!"

At last the taxi stopped and the driver opened the door. "Is this it?" and, as soon as they were out on the pavement, "It is. It is!" cried Li-la, because, facing them were two big plate glass windows lettered in red Chinese writing — both she and Malcolm knew what that was — lit by lamps with long red tassels like the lamps at home; through the glass they could see tables and chairs. Best of all, each side of a red front door were two Fu-dogs, bigger than Malcolm, a hundred times bigger than Fu-dog. They were made of stone, turquoise blue, had no fur ruffs or fur on their ears or tails but each had Fu-dog's great eyes, his teeth and smile and, under a paw, each had the ball of the world.

"My brothers," said Fu-dog proudly.

"It *must* be our restaurant," said Li-la.

"There then." The taxi-driver was pleased but, standing on the pavement, a horrid fact had come to Malcolm; taxis had to be paid for and, if four pence had not been enough to buy anything from the buffet car, it certainly was not enough to pay a taxi. Malcolm, going red again, bravely took out his purse. "We've only got..." he began, but the taxi-driver had leant forward and, with his finger, touched Fu-dog's head and sent it wagging. "Weirdy, isn't he?" he said, then seeing

the purse, "That's all right, son. Keep your pennies."

"How did he know we only had pennies?" Malcolm marvelled.

It was only when the kind taxi-driver had driven away that Malcolm, Li-la and Fu-dog saw that the red front door was shut. Not only shut; when Malcolm tried it, it was locked.

"Of course," said Malcolm. "It's four o'clock. Restaurants open for lunch, then shut till dinner time."

"How long is it till dinner time?" Li-la asked the two Fu-dogs – after all, her own Fu-dog could speak – but they stared straight in front of them. "We'll have to wait," said Malcolm.

"What time is it?" asked Li-la.

"Half-past four."

"What time is it?" she asked – it seemed ages later.

"Twenty to five."

"Fu-dog, you must be cold," but Fu-dog seemed content. "I have my ruff, and it is 'Admiring the Snowflakes Day'," he told Li-la.

"What time is it now?"

"Ten to five."

By five o'clock they were both shivering. Li-la's legs ached terribly; the pavement was so hard it made their feet hurt; Fu-dog had stopped admiring snowflakes but it was half-past five before Li-la suddenly said, "There are people inside. I can see them through the glass."

The children could only see dimly because the inside of the restaurant was not lit but, "They're putting flowers on the tables," said Li-la peering in. "Malcolm, knock."

The red door had a big brass knocker but no bell. Malcolm knocked and knocked. The people inside took no more notice than the Fu-dogs. Malcolm banged on the window but his fists made only a small thudding on the glass and nobody turned a head. "If only we could go *in*," sighed Li-la.

"You can't, but I can," said Fu-dog.

"How can he?" asked Malcolm when Li-la translated. "How?"

Fu-dog's pearl eyes seemed to have swivelled and were pointing to a small open slit in the door. "Through *that*?" asked Malcolm. "That's a letter box."

"Tell him I could be a letter," said Fu-dog. "I mean a message. Write a message and tie it round my neck and I'll take it in."

Malcolm tore a page from his train-spotting notebook, took out his stub of pencil. "Tell him he had better put Li-la not Malcolm," said Fu-dog. "Great Uncle may not know Malcolm's name."

Malcolm was in a huff when Li-la told him.

"Write it yourself," he said.

"You know I don't write very well and I can't spell," but Malcolm put the paper and pencil on one of the stone Fu-dog's head and walked away up the street.

"What can I do?" wailed Li-la. "What can I do?"

"Try," said Fu-dog and Li-la tried.

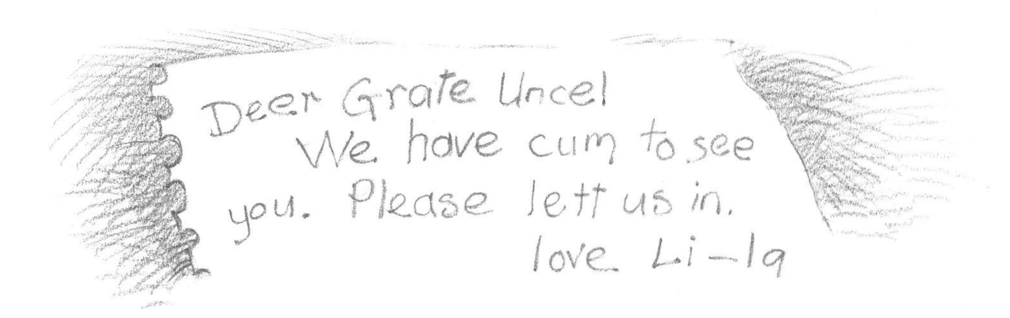

At least she knew how to write that. "Wah!" said Fu-dog. She tied the message round Fu-dog's neck with her hair ribbon.

"They probably won't notice him." Malcolm had come back.

"Everybody notices me," said Fu-dog.

Li-la hoped he was right. Fearfully she pushed him head first, through the letter box; sure enough, almost at once a young man opened the door.

"Yess?"

He was Chinese, young and thin, almost a boy, in black trousers and a white starched coat. Fu-dog, wagging, was in his hand, "Iss yours?" he asked. "Yess?"

"Yess," said Li-la. She could not help speaking like the young man. "Yess."

"What you want?"

"To see our Great Uncle."

"Great Uncle?"

"Yes. He's our Great Uncle, Chinese like you."

"You mean, Mr. Wu?"

Malcolm and Li-la looked at one another. Was that Great Uncle's name? Mr. Wu? Malcolm was not sure but Li-la had seen Fu-dog nodding as hard as he could in the young man's hand and, "Yess," she cried, "Great Uncle Wu."

"Pleasse to come inside," and the young man gave a small bow.

At last they were in, standing in the restaurant's big red-walled room full of tables, chairs and tall screens carved with dragons. There was a red carpet under their feet; the tables had white cloths but were set in a way Malcolm and

Li-la had never seen; each had a vase of flowers, but no knives, forks, spoons or glasses; instead at every place were two slender sticks of pale polished wood held by a green paper band. To show they are new, thought Li-la. "Chopsticks," hissed Malcolm. "I won't use them." Li-la thought they were pretty. Chinese waiters in white coats like the young man's were standing everywhere: there was a quiet sound of bustle and business and a warm smell of cooking, all kinds of smells. "*Please*," said Li-la, "could I sit on a chair?"

"Pleasse ssit," said the young man. "I'll fetch Mr. Wu."

"*You're* not Great Uncle."

"Great Uncle's a business man. He wears business clothes," Malcolm had told Li-la over and over again; she had never believed him, yet who was this?

The young man had come back, bowed – he had beautiful manners – and stood aside for a short plump gentleman in black pin-striped trousers and a black coat; he was wearing horn-rimmed spectacles and his skin was like Li-la's, the creamy-yellow tinged with pink of a white-heart cherry. He was smiling. "Malcolm! Li-la! But *how*?" and he opened his arms.

Malcolm had stood up politely but Li-la had got off her chair and was standing trembling from head to foot. "*You're* not Great Uncle. Where's your blue robe? Where's your beard?" she demanded. "Where's everything? The flower trees?" – she was speaking so fast it came out in a jumble. "The pink roofs, the pool and the bridge? The temple? The p-p-pagodas," she was beginning to sob. "Where's Chinatown? I hate London. I hate it. I'm so tired and cold. Where *is*

Great Uncle?" and Li-la flung herself into Mr. Wu's arms and cried. She cried and cried and cried.

Malcolm looked at the floor. Fu-dog nodded in pity, the young man made a sympathetic clucking noise, the waiters stopped and stared but Mr. Wu patted Li-la gently until the worst of the crying was over; then he took a cream silk handkerchief out of his breast pocket and gently dried her tears.

4

"I am not Great Uncle!" said Mr. Wu. "I am Uncle."

"Uncle? Mum's Big Brother!"

"Yes. Great Uncle is in his house."

"In Chinatown?" Li-la was still having small hiccoughs of tears, "Ch-Chinatown?"

"Perhaps, yes. I will take you to see him by and by." The way Wu-Uncle – that was what it seemed he was – said 'by and by' was like a sing-song and soothing. "I must telephone your mother. She'll be anxious but first…you must be hungry," said Wu-Uncle.

"*Yes!*" Malcolm and Li-la said it together.

Wu-Uncle beamed. "I will order an early supper. Tsan will bring it to you," and Wu-Uncle said something in quick words to the young man – it was the first time Malcolm and Li-la had heard anyone speak Chinese. Tsan bowed. "Tsan has only now come to England," said Wu-Uncle.

"From China?" and, as Tsan disappeared behind a screen, Li-la looked after him with wonder.

"There's one good thing about living in a restaurant," Malcolm was to say. "There's always plenty of food."

Tsan had put a menu on the table, a long menu, with Chinese lettering on the cover, English inside it; as he read it Malcolm's eyes grew bigger and bigger and more and more alarmed.

"Bang bang chicken..."

"That sounds lovely," said Li-la but, "Squid," read Malcolm. "That's octopus. Salt and pepper fried frogs' legs. Ugh." Li-la had to say "ugh," too.

"Tiger's whiskers?" Li-la's eyes, too, grew almost round.

"That's only pork shreds," Malcolm read further.

"Let's ask for that," said Li-la. Malcolm was still shuddering, and when Tsan brought a large tray filled with bowls which, as he lifted the lids, steamed with succulent smells, each one different, "I won't eat anything at all," declared Malcolm.

"It's not frogs' legs," Li-la was sure. "It's what Mum said," fried rice: a dark green sort of vegetable that Li-la guessed was seaweed – it tasted delicious and was crispy. Prawns in batter which she found she liked. "Egg fuey," said Tsan which were eggs in sauce with noodles. She started to eat at once but Malcolm still looked and sniffed.

"You no like?" Tsan was anxious.

"I like English fish and chips," Malcolm was gruff. To his surprise, Tsan whisked his plate away. "I get," he said and, before Li-la had finished her first bowl, Malcolm had a big plate of his favourite fried fish and chips, as hot and crisp as even Mum made them. Malcolm though was still being difficult.

Li-la, delighted, was using chopsticks. Tsan had shown her how to hold them but, "I'm not going to," said Malcolm. Tsan brought forks and knives and spoons so quickly that Malcolm had to be ashamed.

"Anyhow you can't eat ice-cream with chopsticks," he said when they reached the ice-cream stage.

"You can," said Fu-dog but of course Malcolm did not hear.

Li-la cut up the ice-cream wafers for dog biscuits but Fu-dog had his eyes on a bowl full of..."It is pork and dumplings, isn't it?" Li-la asked Tsan.

"Yess."

"Wah!" said Fu-dog, and wagged and wagged.

Wu-Uncle came back.

"Is Mum very cross?" asked Malcolm.

"She hasn't had time to be cross, she has only now come in for-tun-ate-ly." Wu-Uncle spoke in the same soft soothing voice.

"And Dad?" Malcolm's voice grew smaller as he thought of Dad but, "He, too, has not come home," said Wu-Uncle and seeing that Malcolm was beginning to worry, "in any case here you are, they cannot take you back, and ass-ur-ed-ly Great Uncle will talk to them both and settle it."

"Great Uncle settles everything." Li-la was feeling much, much happier. "He sent us Fu-dog and Fu-dog brought us here."

"*Fu-dog* brought us." Malcolm was on the point of being difficult again when there was a sudden deep resounding noise from the street, a noise that echoed on and on; then two such loud bangs that the children jumped almost out of their chairs, "What was that noise?"

Wu-Uncle laughed. "That was a Chinese gong and those loud bangs were fire-crackers."

"Fire-crackers?"

"Fireworks to frighten bad spirits away," Fu-dog nodded. "It's lucky you came tonight," said Wu-Uncle, beaming again. "It is our Chinese New Year celebration," and now the children saw that the street outside the restaurant was full of people, all laughing and shouting and walking. Some carried paper-lanterns lit and glowing, some torches and flares; banners in scarlet and yellow were carried and some of the boys had sticks holding fishes made of blown-up paper, with brilliant paper scales. The girls had hand-rattles and there was a strange kind of music, the gong beat again and there were more fire-crackers. "Oh, can't we go out and see?"

"I am taking you," said Wu-Uncle, "but first you must get dressed."

"Dressed?" They stared. Then, "In Chinese clothes?" Li-la had guessed and clapped her hands.

"Cer-tain-ly. Most people don't but, in our family, it is old tradition for the children. Come upstairs and see. Tsan's mother, Mrs. Ling, has come to England with him and brought his two little sisters."

Tsan's mother and his two little sisters were as plump as Tsan was slim. Mrs. Ling's face beamed as much as Wu-Uncle's; she was rosy, dressed in black trousers and a long black tunic, her hair twisted into a bun and stuck with pins that had flowers and butterflies on their tips. The little sisters wore trousers too, and short padded tunic coats; their hair was tied in bunches with scarlet ribbons; they had little embroidered shoes. Their names were A-kuei and A-lo; A-kuei was seven, like Li-la, A-lo only four. When they saw Li-la, they laughed and laughed, screwing up their slanted eyes so that the eyes almost disappeared and their plumpness shook. They could not talk to her, nor she to them, but soon she was laughing too.

Mrs. Ling brought out clothes; for Li-la a pair of pink silk trousers tied with a scarlet cord, and a padded pink silk coat: for Malcolm a robe of plum-coloured cloth, the sleeves turned back with blue, and a hat of fur and satin. "No thank you," said Malcolm.

"We don't wear them every day," Wu-Uncle coaxed. "Nor-mal-ly A-kuei and A-lo wear clothes like you, but this is gala."

Malcolm still said, "No thank you."

"Malcolm, *please* won't you wear them," Li-la whispered.

"And look a fool?"

"Fu-dog says Tsan didn't look a fool," said Li-la.

"Fu-dog should stay here and not come," said Malcolm.

"Stuff!" said Fu-dog.

Malcolm and Li-la had thought bonfire night in St. Mary's Green was crowded, noisy and exciting but they had never imagined anything like this Chinese New Year.

As they came out — Malcolm wearing his cords and anorak — hundreds of people were standing on the pavement, hundreds more walking or dancing in the procession that was now coming along the street and taking up all the road. The children's eyes were dazzled by the lights; the noise was deafening, gongs, music, voices shouting and singing, while fire-crackers seemed to be exploding under their feet and on every side. They could hardly walk along; Wu-Uncle had A-lo up on his shoulders, Mrs. Ling held A-kuei. Tsan was behind Malcolm and Li-la but it was Malcolm who firmly held Li-la's hand; her other hand clutched Fu-dog and she tried to hold him up so that he could see. "It's *his* New Year," she told Malcolm.

They found a narrow space on the edge of the pavement where they could see the dancing men and boys whirling and jumping, wearing masks and carrying sticks. With Wu-Uncle they stood, dazed and dazzled, too excited to be cold, watching while Mrs. Ling, Tsan, A-kuei, A-lo and Fu-dog gave soft "Wahs", until Li-la felt Fu-dog suddenly stiffen. His eyes came out on their stalks, his head wagged harder than ever and, "Wah! Look! What's *that*?" shrilled Li-la.

An enormous monster was coming, carried high above the crowd; Wu-Uncle told them afterwards there might be ten men inside it. It wriggled and bounced and billowed as the men jumped up and down, its huge head wagging from side to side, its eyes blazing as its tongue lolled out. "Wah!" shouted the crowd. "Wah!" shouted Tsan. "Ace!" breathed Malcolm then suddenly shouted, "Wah! Wah!"

Malcolm says 'Wah!' Fu-dog says 'Stuff!' Topsy-turvy again, thought Li-la.

Little A-lo had given a scream and clutched Wu-Uncle's head. "It's all right. All right." Wu-Uncle patted her as he had patted Li-la, "He's only paper."

His, or its, paper was painted in gaudy colours but its big teeth and fangs were white, the great tongue scarlet. Its eyes were like headlamps. "Wah!" cried Tsan and, "Wah!" shouted the crowd. A-kuei had hidden behind Mrs. Ling, A-lo clung to Wu-Uncle but Li-la did not have a tremor of fear because, "He's a Fu-dog," she cried. "Fu-dog, you *can* really be as big as the sky."

"My other self," said Fu-dog.

"Of course," Wu-Uncle had bent down to talk into Li-la's ear. "In China every year is the year of an animal: this year is the Year of the Dog and Fu-dog has come to bless us."

"I shall be pleased," said Li-la's Fu-dog.

Now the monster Fu-dog was over them in a commotion of noise, treading and dancing. The crowd jostled and surged forward so that the children could hardly stand. Trying not to let them be toppled over, Tsan tightened his grip on them but, at that moment, a man's sleeve, flying as he bent and whirled, caught Li-la's hand so hard that she opened it; Fu-dog was swept off and fell headlong among the dancing feet.

Li-la shrieked and struggled. Tsan held her fast but Malcolm wrenched himself free and, without waiting a moment, dived after Fu-dog into the crowd. Next moment he was knocked down.

Tsan dared not let go of Li-la. Wu-Uncle with A-lo was hemmed in by the crowd and helpless as the dancing feet in boots and shoes trampled over Malcolm. The men inside the monster could not see where they were going and had no idea they were treading down a boy. Malcolm was kicked and tossed and trampled. A policeman in the crowd saw him and dived in himself but he too was knocked over. He lost his helmet but managed to drag Malcolm free and lift him out as Wu-Uncle, who had dumped A-lo in Mrs. Ling's free arm, fought his way to them.

Malcolm was senseless, filthy; one arm was dangling. The monster had passed; other policemen came. Mrs. Ling, A-kuei, A-lo, Tsan and Li-la stood shocked into stillness as two men in uniform brought a stretcher. The policeman and Wu-Uncle laid Malcolm on it. Next moment an ambulance siren was heard shrilling through the streets.

5

Li-la cried herself to sleep. When she woke next morning she began to cry again and went on crying though Wu-Uncle patted her and talked in his beautiful sing-song, though Tsan brought her a special breakfast, Mrs. Ling gave her sweets and A-kuei and A-lo brought her all their toys. She still cried.

"Malcolm's all right," Wu-Uncle told her over and over again. "I stayed with him in the hospital until he went to sleep." Malcolm's arm was broken, he was cut and bruised and sore but, "*He's* eating his breakfast," Wu-Uncle told her now. "I've rung up the hospital. This afternoon we shall bring him home."

Li-la cried.

"Your mum's coming today," said Wu-Uncle, "and your dad."

"Dad?" For a moment Li-la's tears dried she was so astonished. "*Dad?*"

"Yes." Wu-Uncle did not say anything more except, "We shall welcome him."

"It isn't Mum and Dad," sobbed Li-la, "it isn't even Malcolm. It's Fu-dog. My Fu-dog."

Tsan had searched all up and down the road, in the gutters, and in the litter bins; not a single silky white hair of Fu-dog had he found. "I'll buy you another," said Wu-Uncle but, "I don't want another," wailed Li-la, "I want *my* Fu-dog," and she put her head down on the table, and cried and cried.

"I think," said Wu-Uncle, "we had better go and see Great Uncle."

"Great Uncle?" The tears stemmed. Li-la lifted her head.

"Li-la," asked Wu-Uncle. "Do you think you could kowtow?"

"Kowtow?"

"Great Uncle is very old," said Wu-Uncle, "and Chinese people are extra polite to old people; the kowtow is the old time proper Chinese greeting when a little girl pays her first respects to her great uncle – besides he likes it. You go down on your knees." Plump as he was and wearing black striped trousers, Wu-Uncle went down on his knees. "No kneeling up, you go right down." Wu-Uncle went right down. "Bend over," Wu-Uncle bent over, "and touch your forehead on the ground." His forehead touched the ground. "Just for a moment," and Wu-Uncle stood up. "That is kowtow."

Malcolm would never do that, thought Li-la, but she said, "I'll kowtow."

It seemed to make it all more important and, sad though she was, Li-la could not help a feeling of joy; she was going to see Great Uncle at last, joy and hope because, in the back of her mind, she had a feeling that somehow Great Uncle would bring back Fu-dog. "Of course he can't," Malcolm would have said. "Fu-dog must have been trampled to bits. I nearly was and I'm much bigger," but, "Great Uncle settles everything," Li-la had said and as she sat in the car, dressed in her Chinese clothes, though her eyes were still swollen from crying, they were shining.

"But it's a *London* house!" Li-la said in dismay.

They had left the busy crowded streets of traffic and Wu-Uncle had driven up a hill where the streets were wider and emptier with big houses on each side, some with high walls around gardens. Wu-Uncle had stopped at one of these, helped Li-la out of the car and opened a high iron-scrolled gate to show a big house with a big front door. "It's a *London* house!"

"Wait," said Wu-Uncle.

The door was opened by a young Chinese who might have been the twin of Tsan. He *was* the twin of Tsan; Wu-Uncle introduced him, "This is Sheng, Tsan's twin brother." Sheng smiled and bowed and would have taken Wu-Uncle's coat and hat but, "I'm not staying," said Wu-Uncle, "only Little Miss."

Li-la was startled. "I'm to see Great Uncle alone?"

"It's you he wants to see."

At first, all Li-la saw was light, sunlight brilliant after the dark corridor Sheng had taken her down before he opened another door and shut it behind her; light was all round her and flowers, and a gentle tinkling sound with the splashing of water and birds singing. As she steadied, she saw she was

standing in a large high room with a polished floor strewn with rugs in delicate colours and that the flowers were in blue and white porcelain pots higher than herself; though it was winter there were small peach trees in blossom and spring flowers, sweet smelling narcissi and pink flowers she knew were azaleas. Then she saw that, opposite her, in a high carved chair that might have been a throne, an old, old man was sitting, his face and hands the colour of ivory exactly like the mandarin at home; he had white hair and a white pointed beard and, "You've got on your blue robe!" breathed Li-la, then remembered she had not made her kowtow.

Shamed, she fell on her knees, too hard, hastily bent over and, as her little pink-trousered bottom rose in the air, knocked her forehead on the polished floor, again far too hard. "Ouch!"

"Ouch!" said Great Uncle.

It *was* 'ouch'. Li-la's head spun with the knock, tears came back into her eyes, and once they had come she could not stop them but Great Uncle seemed to understand. "Tell me," he said – he had drawn her to his chair – "Tell me," and Li-la told, from the very beginning when Fu-dog had come to their home in St. Mary's Green, until the New Year of the Dog in London and, "Fu-dog's gone," Li-la began sobbing even more. "I'll never have him again. Great Uncle, you weren't anywhere, and there isn't a Chinatown."

"Come with me," said Great Uncle.

They were in a garden, or a garden of gardens, like a little town. "Chinatown!" whispered Li-la. Against the London wall of his London house, Great Uncle had built a Chinese summer house, a pavilion with bamboo lattices and here were the tip-tilted curled up roofs, though the tiles were black, not pink. Paths led away to other gardens cunningly hidden, zig-zag paths because Chinese people think straight paths bring bad luck. Here was the little bridge across a pool; though the pool did not have a boat it had fish swimming with golden fins and a little waterfall splashed. The tinkling sound Li-la had heard were Chinese wind-chimes, thin strips of glass hung up so that they tinkled against one another when the wind blew.

One garden had a pagoda, not very high but hung with

bells; another had a tree that in spite of the January cold, was in perfect blossom. "If it doesn't flower I cheat," Great Uncle whispered as if the tree could hear. "I light braziers of hot coals underneath it; they get so warm, it has to flower." He chuckled. "Don't tell anyone," he whispered.

"I won't," Li-la whispered back.

All the gardens had names; Great Uncle told them to Li-la as they walked hand in hand: The Garden of Quietness had a stone bench for sitting on, "and doing nothing but dream," said Great Uncle: The Pavilion for Smelling Roses had another smaller summer house and was planted with roses. The Place to Admire the Plum Blossom was the garden that had the flowering tree. The bridge was The Bridge of the Little Flying Rainbows because, he said, the waterfall made rainbows on sunny days: The Pigeon Garden had a dovecote but there were no pigeons. "I had white fantails," said Great Uncle. "We used to tie small pipes under their wings so that when they flew the pipes made music, but cats got my pigeons." So Great Uncle had his sadness too and that reminded Li-la.

"Great Uncle," she said. "Where is Fu-dog?" An odd question to ask when she knew, as Malcolm had said, that Fu-dog had been trampled and stamped to bits—mysteriously now, with Great Uncle, she was able to say 'Fu-dog' without crying.

Great Uncle took a little time to answer, then, "Fu-dog was a spirit dog," said Great Uncle, "and spirits come and go."

"But...do they go and come?" asked Li-la.

"In all sorts and sizes," said Great Uncle.

Tired of walking, they were sitting on the bench in The

Garden of Quietness and now Li-la remembered something else.

"Great Uncle," she said, "is it true that everything you touch turns to gold?"

"Some things," said Great Uncle. "A kind of gold. Some things." His voice when he said 'some things' was like Wu-Uncle's when he had said 'by and by', a sing-song so soothing that Li-la was able to gather herself together and ask the question she really wanted to ask. "If you had touched Fu-dog would he have turned" – and she remembered the words – "into a golden-coated nimble dog?"

"Perhaps I have," said Great Uncle, and he said, "Li-la, clap your hands."

Li-la clapped obediently. Sheng appeared. "Bring the basket," ordered Great Uncle.

The basket was shaped like a little house with a latticed window. Sheng put it down at Li-la's feet.

"Kneel down."

"Do you mean kowtow?" Li-la was ready to kowtow.

"If you like," so Li-la kowtowed. She was to remember that kowtow all her life.

"Now open it."

Sheng had undone the straps, Li-la lifted the roof lid – and stopped. "Oh no!" she whispered. "I can't believe it! I can't." Then, "Oh *yes!*" There, curled on a blanket of the palest blue, was a tiny dog – a puppy of a kind she hadn't seen before, and she seemed to hear Fu-dog's voice:

'Let the dog be small.'

The puppy was small.

'Let it have a ruff around its neck.'

There was the beginning of a ruff.

'Let its coat be plentiful.'

At present it was close and silky, "It has to grow," said Great Uncle.

'Let its tail fall like a chrysanthemum...'

What Li-la could see of it, the puppy's tail was more like a tadpole's. "It has to grow," said Great Uncle.

'Let its eyes be dark, large and shining.'

"Oh, they are! They are!" whispered Li-la.

'Let it be friendly.'

In answer to that, when Li-la put out her hand to stroke the puppy gently, gently, it put out a little pink tongue and licked her finger.

"Is he yours?" she whispered to Great Uncle.

"I rather think," said Great Uncle, "he is yours."

"What are you going to call him?" asked Mum. There was only one name, Fu. "Fu the Second," said Mum.

Mum and Dad had arrived that afternoon.

Wu-Uncle had met them; they had fetched Malcolm from the hospital and come to the restaurant where Li-la, Tsan, Mrs. Ling, A-kuei, A-lo and all the waiters were waiting. "Please don't let them be pernickity," Li-la was whispering. "Please don't let Dad be rough and ready," but it was the happiest of meetings and Dad had brought some beautiful pots of jam, particularly apricot, as 'lucky money' to bring luck to the Wu and Ling families in the New Year.

Mum did say, "You were very naughty children," but had to add, "I'm glad you were."

Wu-Uncle gave a supper in his private room, dish after dish. "All the lovely things I have missed so much," said Mum.

"It's good!" said Dad in such surprise that everybody laughed as he tried the restaurant's prawns and crispy fried duck.

"I thought you didn't like Chinese food," Wu-Uncle teased him.

"I have to eat my words," said Dad.

Li-la stared. Could anyone eat words? There seemed no end to the strange things grown-ups could do.

Tsan had brought Malcolm his special plate of fish and chips but now Malcolm stretched out his good hand and took one of Dad's prawns, then another and when Mrs. Ling put rice, egg fuey and chicken in front of him he ate that too. "Do you think I could have some Tiger's Whiskers?" he asked.

"Of course you can," said Mrs. Ling. "You can have anything you want, my brave boy." Malcolm was pale and stiff. His arm was in plaster and a sling; one eye was half-closed, swollen with bruises, and he had patches of plaster on his cuts. "Malcolm's a hero," said Mrs. Ling and everyone raised their glasses of wine or little bowls of green Chinese tea.

"Master Malcolm is a hero."

Li-la and Malcolm were sitting by themselves at the far end of the table and Malcolm lifted his head. "That's Fu-dog's voice."

"Fu-dog?" Li-la sat up too.

"...a hero." It was distinct.

"It *is* Fu-dog. I heard him," she cried. Then, in wonder, "Malcolm! You heard him too."

"Of course I heard him. I heard him before. Why else do you think I went into that crowd? You were shrieking too much to hear but I heard him. Fu-dog called me, me, not you. 'Malcolm! Help, Malcolm! Save me. Malcolm, Malcolm, save me,' and I didn't," said Malcolm. "I couldn't." He pushed his plate away in misery.

"Wu-Uncle," Li-la said in a loud voice, extraordinarily loud for her. "Wu-Uncle, please. Please can Malcolm and I go to see Great Uncle?"

"What? Now?" Wu-Uncle was startled.

"Now," and Li-la stood up. When Wu-Uncle looked at Malcolm he stood up too.

"I'll come with you," said Mum.

"No. Only Malcolm." Li-la did not know why she was so certain it must be only Malcolm but, "You keep Fu-puppy for me," she said and gave the warm little bundle to Mum.

At Great Uncle's, Malcolm did not go any further than the big light room of flowers and colours. He did not need to. "Great Uncle never wastes time," said Li-la.

"Good evening, boy."

"Good evening, Great Uncle."

Malcolm had not kowtowed but bowed like Tsan and Sheng; then stood as tall as he could in front of the carved chair. Li-la had gone straight to Great Uncle.

"I am glad to see you." Great Uncle told Malcolm and he said, "Some people got medals for bravery. In old China it used to be a Sword of Honour." Malcolm wondered what he could do with a Sword of Honour in St. Mary's Green. "But I thought," said Great Uncle, "you would rather have this." He clapped his hands and, as if Sheng had been waiting, he wheeled in a bicycle. "O-ooh!" breathed Li-la because it was the bicycle Malcolm had dreamed of and saved up for so

long in his china pig; a red bicycle, its chrome gleaming silver, with white tyres, three-speed gears and a pump. "Is it the right one?" asked Great Uncle but, as Malcolm bent over it, touched it, he could only nod, he could not speak.

Then, as if he had remembered something, he stood up and flushed red. "Great Uncle, you're great but... I mustn't have it. I didn't save Fu-dog. I tried but I couldn't. I couldn't."

"Of course you couldn't," said Great Uncle. "How could you? The time had come for Fu-dog to join his ancestors."

"Ancestors?" asked Li-la.

"All the Fu-dogs who had been here before him. On one day, every year, we Chinese honour our ancestors so that we never forget them. We bring flowers and lights for them and burn little sticks of sweet smelling incense called joss sticks."

"Could we get some joss sticks?" asked Malcolm.

"You don't need them yet," said Great Uncle. "Listen."

"Master Malcolm is a hero." It was Fu-dog's voice, again quite distinct.

"You see," said Great Uncle.

"Master Malcolm is a hero."

Though Malcolm liked 'Master' he had to say, "Stuff!"

"It isn't stuff," said Li-la. "It's Wah," and "Wah!" echoed Fu-dog and again, though it was getting fainter, "Wah."

"Wah!" said Great Uncle, Malcolm and Li-la all together.

Dad, Mum, Malcolm, Li-la, the dream bicycle and, of course the Peking puppy, Fu, went back to St. Mary's Green but everything was different. "Wu-Uncle pernickity? Who said so?" asked Dad; as for 'rough and ready' – "Your daddy is a perfect English gentleman," Mrs. Ling told Li-la. Sometimes now Mum cooked Chinese food, especially pork with dumplings and when Wu-Uncle, Mrs. Ling, Tsan, A-kuei and A-lo said Li-la must come back and stay with them every year, "Can I come too?" asked Malcolm but Li-la was puzzled. "Stay with them?" she asked. To her it seemed as if she had never gone away. She had only to shut her eyes, anytime, anywhere, and she seemed to be with Great Uncle in his Chinatown garden again; she saw the pool, the bridge, and the fish, the plum tree in blossom, the little pagoda but, particularly, The Garden of Quietness.

"Great Uncle, is it true that everything you touch turns to gold?"

"Some things. Some things," she could hear Great Uncle's sing-song. "A kind of gold."

Fu grew fast: his tail began to look more like a chrysanthemum, his coat like gold spun silk: he was lively and gambolled and he was Fu-dog over again. "Too big for his paws," said Malcolm. "Look how he goes bouncing up to huge dogs — even a Great Dane!"

"Because he *is* Fu-dog." Li-la believed that firmly. "Great Uncle touched him."

"How?" said Malcolm.

"I don't know how, but somehow." Li-la believed that too. "I'll never forget my Fu-dog the First," said Li-la. "Never."

"But he was hideous," Malcolm had to say.

"Beautiful," said Li-la.